COLLISION
in Columbia

by
Phil Hardwick

QUAIL RIDGE PRESS
Brandon, Mississippi

Other books in Phil Hardwick's Mississippi Mysteries Series:

Found in Flora

Justice in Jackson

Captured in Canton

Newcomer in New Albany

Vengeance in Vicksburg

To be included on the Mississippi Mysteries mailing list, please send your name and complete mailing address to:

QUAIL RIDGE PRESS
P. O. Box 123 • Brandon, MS 39043
1-800-343-1583

DEDICATION

*Dedicated to the memory of
Hugh Lawson White,
father of economic and community
development in Mississippi.*

Preface / Acknowledgments

Dear Reader:

Welcome to Number Six in the Mississippi Mysteries Series. I hope you enjoy reading it as much as I enjoyed writing it. The best part of my task as an author is meeting the people in each town I write about and getting to know the history of their community. Recently, someone remarked to me that when all is said and done, every town is the same. I disagree. Every place has its own unique character and history. That is what makes every place different.

In getting to know the people of Columbia, I was struck by how many achievers hail from this little city on the Pearl River. Without a doubt, the late Hugh Lawson White, former Mayor of Columbia and Governor of Mississippi, is the city's most prominent public servant and business owner. Anyone involved in community and economic development should study his life. In the world of sports, football greats Walter Payton and Eagle Day both hail from Columbia. There are many others.

The Board of Directors of the Columbia Main Street program were especially helpful. Judy Griffith, the Executive Director, spent many hours showing me around and answering questions. Main Street in Columbia really is a special place. By the way, all of the places mentioned in Columbia really do exist, and I encourage you to visit them. On the other hand, all of the characters exist only in my imagination.

Finally, there really are white squirrels in Columbia.

Phil Hardwick

Chapter 1

It all began as a minor traffic accident on Main street. It was a clear, cool Thanksgiving Thursday afternoon, and downtown Columbia was almost deserted except for the two cars at the traffic signal at Main Street and 2nd Street. When the light turned green, the Corvette pulled away at a slow speed, heading up Main Street away from the courthouse. The second car accelerated as normal. Suddenly the Corvette stopped as if to avoid an animal, and was smacked in the rear by the other car.

As the last piece of the broken parking light fell to the pavement with a tinkling sound, the driver's door of the Corvette swung open and a lanky man somewhere around fifty years old extricated himself from the low-slung car. He wore dress cowboy boots, pressed blue jeans, a pale blue shirt and a blue sports coat. He walked to the rear of his car, bent over at the waist and inspected the condition of the two vehicles at the point of collision. There was no evidence whatsoever of a collision on the rear of the Corvette, but the Buick sustained slight damage to its grille and a broken parking light. He turned toward the driver of the Buick and moved toward her. Margaret Carswell just sat there, her 73-year old hands in a death grip on the steering wheel. Her heart was racing as the man approached. With her left hand, she opened the door, but remained seated.

"Ma'am, I'm so sorry," said the man apologetically

in an accent that said he had grown up out in the country. "This was all my fault."

"Oh, no," replied Ms. Carswell, catching her breath. "I was the one who rear-ended you. The one who does the rear-ending is always at fault. I should have been watching more closely."

"With all due respect, that's ridiculous. My cellular telephone rang and I slammed on brakes to answer it. It really was my fault." He pushed the side of his blue coat back, reached into the front pocket of his jeans, and produced a wad of bills folded in half and held together by a gold money clip. He peeled off a one hundred dollar bill and handed it to her. "Here, take this for the trouble I caused. It should be enough to repair your damage."

"I'm sorry," she replied as her jaw raised. "I cannot accept money for something that was my fault. It's kind of you to offer."

"Please. It's the least I can do."

"I should be offering you money," she said, reaching for her purse.

"Ma'am, as you see, there's no damage to my car. I couldn't take any money from you."

"Well, I want to do what's right."

"So do I," he said slowly. "So do I." He turned around, got back in the sleek sports car, and drove north out of town, the guttural sound of the exhaust pipes fading away.

It took her almost an hour to get over it. She had

never had a traffic accident in her life. After recovering from the incident, Margaret Carswell thought little more of it for the rest of the day. Her mind was preoccupied with something else.

For the first time in over fifty years, the Thanksgiving meal had not been held at her home. Her son had insisted that it be held at his house so that she wouldn't have to do all the preparation and hostess duties. Her children did not understand that what she liked about the day was all the fuss in the kitchen and the dining room. Perhaps they thought they were doing her a favor. But she knew better. They had taken one more tradition from the Carswell family. She also took it as one more sign that they thought she was getting old. Which was false as could be! She had never felt better in her life.

It was true that Margaret Carswell's life was changing. Her friends and acquaintances were dying off. Every morning she walked out to the end of her driveway, picked up *The Columbian Progress,* went back to her kitchen table, and with a warm cup of hot chocolate in her hand, scanned the obituary section. Hardly a week went by that she did not find the name of someone she knew.

It had been ten years since her husband, John Carswell, died of a heart attack in his sleep the day after his sixty-fourth birthday. Her life with him had been good. They were high school sweethearts, and had planned on getting married as soon as possible after graduation from Columbia High School. Their parents had other plans. Seeing the infatuation between the young boy and girl, their parents sent them in opposite directions. John went north to Ole Miss to college, while Margaret was forced to go to Tulane in New Orleans. It was not a good experience for her, and was made bearable only by the daily letters she received from John. While at home in Columbia on Christmas recess, she and John schemed about a way to elope to Alabama and get married. They would have carried out their plan, too, had not their parents finally relented and reached a compromise. Margaret could go to school at Mississippi State College for Women in Columbus, Mississippi. It was closer to Ole Miss, but not too close. She accepted the proposition and completed her collegiate matriculation there. John visited her as often as possible, but their lives apart were tortuous. They were as in love as any two people could have been. After college they were married in the United Methodist Church in Columbia and, as they say in the fairy tales, "lived happily ever after."

Now she was alone. Not only was she alone, she was growing old. People were treating her differently. With more deference. With more condescension. Her son and daughter, John, Jr. and Joanna, seemed to be actively doing all they could to make her feel old, useless, and like they were anxious to have her out of their lives. When they telephoned her, they would ask things like: "Do we need to get a sitter for you?" and "Have you considered how much fun it would be to live in one of those retirement centers?" Last week, John, Jr. had even asked if she had renewed her driver's license. "They make you take a test again if you forget to renew it," he had said with a twinge of sarcasm. What did he know? She could drive as well as he could!

Nevertheless, she had just run into the back of another car. If she had been younger, would she have been paying more attention? Were they right? They were probably already picking out a nursing home for her. She would seek advice on Monday from the only person she truly trusted. Her children were not going to take advantage of her.

Chapter 2

The following Monday morning she got in her car and drove the few, short blocks to Main Street and Hill Hardware, where she worked on a part-time, as-needed basis. With Christmas only a few weeks away, she was needed a lot these days. She wore a dark blue dress with brass buttons, a gray, heavy cotton scarf around her neck, and a long, blue overcoat to protect her from the chilly, early morning air. By noon, the temperature would be in the low seventies, a typical late November Mississippi day. She went inside the store, put on a smile, and prepared to greet customers.

At Hill Hardware Company, the past and present can be found side by side. The business was incorporated on Christmas Eve, 1901, by the Hill family of Mobile, Alabama, and was then located a few doors down from its present spot at 717 Main Street. Cause for the relocation was a fire in 1916. Back in 1901, the emporium sold everything a turn-of-the-century household could possibly need, including hubs, spokes and axles for wagons, china, crockery, silverware, seed, clothing and groceries. Butter churns and molds, cast iron stoves and cookware were stocked then and are still available today. The first gasoline pump in Columbia was located at Hill Hardware, and the store sold the first Ford automobile in the area.

Today the store stocks approximately 24,000 items

and has a "want book" for customers to order anything not in stock. The owner is quick to point out, however, that "If we don't have it, then you probably don't need it." Hill Hardware is the only store in the area that sells syrup cans, and still sells over 400 cases per year of 50 cans to the case. Regular patrons come from Jackson, New Orleans, and the Mississippi Gulf Coast just to shop at the unique retail outlet. More than a few ask, "Is Maggie working today?" Just last week she sold over $1,200 worth of Hill Hardware's old-time cotton baskets to a couple from Houston, Texas, who were starting a restaurant in an old cotton mill.

By 10:30 Maggie was ready for her morning break. She walked out to the back alley and strode a few doors down to the Back Door Cafe where she met her youth-

ful soulmate, Lindsey Plummer, the person she trusted most. At the counter, they both ordered hot chocolate.

"Are you going to work every day this season?" asked Margaret, as they sat down at a table.

"All day, every day until Christmas Eve, Miss Maggie," Lindsey replied, blowing the top of her cup to speed up the cooling of her chocolate.

"Lindsey, please stop calling me Miss Maggie. It makes me feel old. Maggie will do just fine. And you, young lady, are going to get old too fast if you work every day like you have been doing."

"I need the extra money," said Lindsey. "Christmas is coming, you know."

Maggie had met Lindsey Plummer three months earlier while the two were sharing a break at this very table at the Back Door Cafe, a small informal restaurant located inside the Lampton Company Department Store, and so named because of its street entrance from the alley behind the store. Lindsey had been sipping a cola and pondering a passage in an English literature textbook when Maggie sat down at the table beside her.

"You look like you aren't enjoying that book," Maggie had said with a mild grin.

"I'm supposed to write a paper on some guy named Bartleby the Scrivener."

"Oh, yes," Maggie had replied. "He's the one who preferred not to do certain things."

"How did you know that?"

"I like to read a lot. I would have made a good

THE BACK DOOR CAFE

English Literature teacher, if I do say so myself. But my husband didn't want me to work."

They hit it off immediately and had such an animated conversation that they were both late getting back from their break that day. Maggie was impressed with the independent youngster, and in a short time the two had become confidants, sharing secrets on their breaks like two teenage girls at a spend-the-night party.

Lindsey was twenty-one years old, but looked seventeen. She had short, golden hair, a slightly turned up nose and blue Bambi-eyes. She had a three-year-old son from a six-month marriage that was wrong from the start. The father left town before the baby was born, leaving Lindsey to make it on her own. Fortunately her divorced mother lived next door and helped take care of the baby while Lindsey worked during the day at Lampton's. Lindsey viewed her situation as only temporary. This past August she had enrolled in the local community college, taking English Lit at night and American Government on Saturday mornings. She made an "A" in both courses, which was no surprise, given the fact that she had made a 28 on her ACT college entrance exam. That score placed her far above the national average. Because of her pregnancy, she did not graduate with her high school class, instead opting for the alternative General Education Diploma. She vowed to become the first person in her family to be a college graduate. Her mother always told her, "Lindsey, all you can do is do the best with what you've got." Lindsey believed this mantra to be true, but she also believed that one could achieve anything if the mind was set to it.

"Was there much damage to your car?" asked Lindsey.

"What are you talking about?" asked Maggie, setting her cup on the table and narrowing her eyebrows.

"Didn't you have a little fender-bender this past weekend on Main Street?" Lindsey teased.

"Well, as a matter of fact, I did. How did you know about a thing like that?"

"I heard it on the radio driving in to work," said Lindsey. "Everybody in town probably knows it by now. A red Corvette, huh?"

"Why that sorry excuse for a radio disc jockey! That's nobody's business."

"Lighten up, Miss Maggie. Main thing is that you're all right." She paused and scanned Margaret Carswell. "You are all right, aren't you?"

"I'm perfectly fine, thank you," she replied, thinking that Lindsey wouldn't have made that comment to a younger person.

"Has it been busy at Hill Hardware this morning?" asked Lindsey.

"Like bees in a hive. I think everybody in town is out shopping today."

"I've already had a half-dozen customers request gift-wrapping," said Lindsey.

"The manager has asked me to work late a lot lately," said Maggie. "He didn't know we were going to have this much business. I can't believe how many people are coming up here from New Orleans." She glanced at her wristwatch. "Oops, got to get going."

They said their farewells and returned to their respective stores. At three, Maggie said good-bye to Hill Hardware and motored the four blocks back to her large Victorian home on Church Street. She drove up the asphalt driveway on the right side of the house, and parked the Buick in the one-car garage in the back yard. She went inside her home, still lamenting that Thanksgiving dinner had not been held here.

Her house held so many special memories. She had raised her children here, entertained her husband's business associates, and hosted many of Columbia's most prominent social events. It was a house well-suited for all those purposes. Victorian in style, with a wide porch that wrapped around the front and side, it was eggshell white, trimmed in rich maroon. There were three large bedrooms, two and a half bathrooms, a large kitchen, two dining rooms and a large living room and parlor styled after the Mississippi Governor's Mansion. She had lived here since she was 25 years old.

She walked to the front door of the house and looked down on the floor where three pieces of mail had come to rest after being shoved through the mail slot in the front door. There was a letter from a retired persons' association, the weekly bulletin from the United Methodist Church, and a white, business-sized envelope with her name and address hand-printed on it, but no return address. She opened it. Inside was a crisp, new one hundred dollar bill and a three-by-five-inch index card on which was printed, "Hope this helps."

Chapter 3

Maggie Carswell studied the envelope. It bore a Hattiesburg, Mississippi postmark over a first-class stamp. "Ms. Margaret Carswell" and her home address were hand-printed in blue ink with a ballpoint pen. There was no return address.

She stared at the envelope for a moment and concluded that it came from the man in the red car last Thursday. It was probably the same hundred dollar bill that he had offered her at the time. She thought to herself that maybe the world wasn't as bad as some say it is these days. She put the money and the index card back in the envelope and placed it in the drawer of a small table in the foyer by the front door. It would find its way to the collection plate of her church on Sunday morning.

Now in a pensive mood, she turned and gazed into the living room. It had been the scene of many a reception and social gathering over the years and was perfectly suited to such events. The twelve-foot high ceiling and seven tall windows made the room feel open and larger than it really was. Two large yellow winged-back sofas, three matching love seats and two chairs were strategically placed in such a manner that receptions flowed smoothly. On the floor was an attractive Oriental rug. A fireplace with a large mantel was centered on the side wall. The fireplace had been fitted with natural gas logs two years ago, and she could control them with a hand-held, remote control device. Above the mantel was a painting of a cypress swamp, with moss-draped trees. Her husband had been given the painting by a lumber buyer in New Orleans. He insisted that it remain there because lumber was his business and brought wealth to the family. She secretly detested it because she preferred paintings with vistas. She liked wide-open views. It suddenly dawned on her—she was a meadow person, and her husband was a woods person. It was a little late to come to that realization. He was gone. It was time to change the painting.

Her thoughts were interrupted by the ringing of the basic beige telephone in the hall.

"Good afternoon, Mom."

"Well, hello, John Junior. How's Columbia's best lawyer today?"

"Mom, I'm not the best lawyer and please call me John. Just John. Daddy died ten years ago."

"People in Columbia still think of him when they hear the name John Carswell. You need your own identity. It was a mistake to tag you with 'Junior' and I told him so. He put that name on the birth certificate without my permission while I was recovering from your delivery."

She was right about the first part and he knew it. Of course, that was precisely the reason he had dropped the "Jr." off his stationery, business cards, telephone listing and every other aspect of his business life after his father's death. He would do just fine with his father's identity. His own was so sadly lacking. It had been a month now since he had had a client walk in the front door of his downtown law office or call on the telephone for that matter.

"How are you feeling today?" he asked.

"I'm fine, thank you," she said clearly. "How are you?"

"Would you like to go to The Brandon House for supper tonight?" he asked. "Sharon and Emily went to Hattiesburg and won't be home until late."

"Is Emily doing another recital?"

"It's a rehearsal," he replied. "The recital is not until Friday night. You know how Sharon has always pushed Emily to play the piano. I guess it's worth it though. Emily is only a freshman majoring in music at the University of Southern Mississippi and she's already doing things that seniors get to do. Hopefully, she will get a scholarship next year."

"Your wife should let her be a regular girl. She pushes Emily too hard. Just like she pushes you, if I may say so."

"Mom. Watch it."

"You know it's true," said Maggie. "We will go to dinner if you promise not to talk to me about my making a will."

"It's something you need to do," he said.

"Your father didn't have a will, and I don't need a will. At least not yet anyway. I don't plan on dying anytime soon."

"Daddy also lost over a third of his estate to the government because of taxes. You don't want that to happen to you, do you?"

"I think I'll pass on dinner," she said with just a touch of frustration.

Maggie hung up the telephone, went to her bedroom, and lay down on her queen-sized bed, which was covered with a quilt that her mother had made over fifty years ago. On the nightstand was a timer, identical to one in the kitchen. She set it for forty minutes, then closed her eyes. A late afternoon nap was becoming a daily necessity.

Chapter 4

Four weeks later, downtown Columbia was bustling with last-minute Christmas shoppers. Although its population was just over 7,000, Columbia drew shoppers from several surrounding counties. The Pearl River, which flows from northeast Mississippi to the Gulf of Mexico, has always played a large role in the history of Columbia and Marion County. Every few dozen years it will leave its banks and remind downtown Columbia of its presence. Nevertheless, the occasional wrath suffered by Columbia, or any river town for that matter, is almost always made up for by the commerce and recreation provided by the waterway. Indeed, Columbia's motto is "City of Charm on the River Pearl."

Columbia, the county seat of Marion County, was originally known as Lott's Bluff, named after an early pioneer family from Georgia who settled in the area between 1805 and 1810. At the time, Mississippi was a territory, becoming a state on December 10, 1817, when President James Monroe signed the document admitting it to the Union as the 20th state. The capitol of Mississippi was Natchez, which was located in the extreme southwestern part of the state on the Mississippi River. Columbia became Mississippi's fourth city by act of the 1818 session of the Legislature. It was named in honor of Columbia, South Carolina, from whence many of its citizens had come. By 1820 a movement was growing to move the State Capitol in Natchez to a more central location. The 1821 session of the Mississippi Legislature, which was only its fourth, ordered that the Capitol be moved to a temporary location until a permanent Capitol could be selected. Columbia was chosen for the distinction, and the next session of the General Assembly met in a three-story frame hotel at Buckhorn Creek, which is just north of the current Water Park. During the session the Poindexter Code was adopted and Governor Walter Leake, Mississippi's third chief executive, was inaugurated.

The most historic building in the area is the John Ford House, which is located in Sandy Hook on State Highway 35 between Bogalusa, Louisiana and Columbia. Believed to be built by a Spanish squatter in 1792, it was purchased by Rev. John Ford in the early 1800's. In 1813 a stockade was built around it and it became a stopping point for many travelers through the region. General Andrew Jackson spent the night there on November 27, 1814 enroute to the Battle of New Orleans. Rev. Ford hosted Methodist Conferences there in 1814 and 1818. In 1971 the home was added to the National Register of Historic Places.

The dominant building in Columbia today is the County Courthouse, which sits at the head of Main Street on a plot of land given by John Lott, one of the town's early settlers. Its clocks can be seen for blocks away. Masons of St. Alban's Lodge No. 60, F&AM laid the cornerstones of the courthouse and the first brick of Columbia High School on the same day in 1905.

With less than a week until Christmas, Main Street was decked out accordingly. At night, lights outlined the buildings, and decorations adorned the windows. There was a cold front headed toward Mississippi and there was talk of the possibility of snow on Christmas Day. Stores bustled with activity. Maggie Carswell was working until six o'clock for the third day in a row. She had already bought presents for her children and grand-children, but this year had added Lindsey Plummer and her young child to the list. At afternoon break time she met Lindsey at the Back Door Cafe as usual. Today the cafe was serving hot spiced apple cider, so they each ordered a cup and claimed their usual table. Lindsey noticed Maggie seemed preoccupied today.

"Lindsey, could you come by my house after work?" asked Maggie with a touch of seriousness.

"Sure, Maggie. Mind if I ask why?"

"You remember that accident back on Thanksgiving weekend?"

"Of course. Wait, don't tell me," said Lindsey. "He's come back and filed a lawsuit against you."

"No," said Maggie. "Nothing like that. Just come by the house and I'll tell you about it."

That evening Lindsey appeared at Maggie's house as promised.

"Sorry, I'm late," she said breathlessly as she removed her multi-colored scarf. "We had to run the customers off at closing time. Everybody's waiting until the last minute this year."

"Come over here and sit down at the table," said Maggie Carswell with a wave of her arm.

Lindsey walked over to a small dining table against the wall opposite the kitchen. On the table in front of her were four business-sized envelopes, each addressed in hand printing to Margaret Carswell at her home address.

"Look in each one," instructed Maggie. "I'll get us some hot chocolate."

Lindsey picked up an envelope and looked inside to find a one hundred dollar bill and a three by five white index card. On the card was printed, "For you." She looked at Maggie with a quizzical look.

"Read each one," Maggie insisted over her shoulder.

Lindsey read them one by one.

"Best Wishes."

"You are in my thoughts."

Maggie placed two cups of steaming hot chocolate on the table, took a seat and said, "Remember the day of my little car accident?"

"Yes," replied Lindsey.

"On the following Monday the first one came. Every Monday since then another one has arrived."

"Wow. What does it mean?"

"I don't know, but I've got to find out. Can you help me?"

"I don't know how I can help," said Lindsey.

"I hope you don't mind my being so personal," she said. "Didn't your mother hire a private detective to find your child's father because he wouldn't make child support payments?"

"Yes," said Lindsey, lowering her head slightly. "She used a man from Jackson. He's a retired police officer and he can find anybody."

"This business of receiving an envelope every Monday is driving me crazy," said Maggie. "I've got to get to the bottom of this. What's the detective's name?"

"Jack Boulder. I'll get you his telephone number tomorrow."

Chapter 5

Jack Boulder finished his morning run and returned to his downtown Jackson condominium. The blinking light on the answering machine summoned his attention. He pushed the appropriate button and listened. He heard the voice of what he would describe as a female senior citizen.

"Yes, uh - hello." She obviously was not accustomed to answering machines. "This is Margaret Carswell in Columbia, Mississippi. Please call me. You were recommended by Lindsey Plummer." Then she left her telephone number.

Boulder paused and recalled the Lindsey Plummer case. It was one that had given him a surprising amount of personal satisfaction. Normally his cases involved criminal activity. He left the divorces and child support cases to rookie private eyes who were trying to get established in the business. After all, he was a retired St. Louis police homicide detective. He usually avoided civil cases. But there had been something about Lindsey Plummer. Perhaps it was her determination and positive attitude about life that influenced his decision. It was what amounted to a missing person case. Her husband had left town, leaving her with a baby and a court order requiring him to pay child support. The jerk had never paid a dime. Boulder found the ex-husband on the Gulf Coast making good money in one of the casinos. The creep was forced to pay back child support and, after a court hearing, was held in contempt. Boulder was pleased with the justice that had been done in the case. Cases like that don't always have a happy ending.

After showering and dressing, he called the Columbia telephone number. Margaret Carswell answered on the second ring.

"You come highly recommended, Mr. Boulder," she said a bit too sternly. "I would like to meet you and discuss my case with you."

"When and where would be convenient?" asked Boulder. He would meet this woman as a favor to Lindsey.

"Noon at the Round Table."

"I'm sorry," he said. "I'm not familiar with the Round Table."

"It's on Church Street. Right off Main," she said. "You can't miss it."

"Ms. Carswell, I'm in Jackson. That's a ways from Columbia."

"You can drive it in an hour and a half with no problem," she said in school teacher fashion. "Is that a problem for you?"

"No, it's just that . . ."

"Good," she said. "I look forward to seeing you at noon."

As he hung up the telephone, he muttered a curse. Why had he let her railroad him into driving to

Columbia? He hadn't even told her what his fee would be or whether he was even interested in the case. He didn't even know what the case was about. After a few minutes of thinking about what to do, he called Lindsey's home in Columbia, but got no answer. What the heck? It was a nice, cool day and he had no other cases pending. Maybe he could find a Christmas present for his girlfriend. It would also be a good day to drive his fully restored 1968 Camaro on the open road.

At 11:45 a.m. he arrived in Columbia and sought out the designated restaurant. The Round Table was located on Church Street in a large, white boarding house with steps leading up to a front porch. It had its beginning in the late 1940's when a desperate widow with three young children opened a boarding house to help make ends meet. Boarders got three meals a day every day except Christmas, and as many as 30 meals a day were sent out to workers who could not leave their jobs. Over the years, boarders at the Round Table reflected the times. After World War II there were returning servicemen, in the oil boom years as many as 20 oil workers slept four to a room, and in the 1970's elderly ladies spent their days in the kitchen laughing, shelling peas and peeling potatoes. Nowadays the boarders are just about gone, but the lunches are as popular as ever. The reputation of the place has spread far and wide and the register lists visitors from almost every state and many foreign countries. What brings them to the Round Table restaurant in Columbia is the Southern cooking presented on the huge Lazy Susan twirling in the center of the table. On a typical day, patrons enjoy fried chicken, peas, chicken and dumplings, cornbread, several casseroles, and a potpourri of desserts.

Boulder entered and told the hostess that he was waiting on someone. "Would that be Ms. Carswell?" asked the woman.

"Yes."

"She's right over there, waiting for you," she said with a smile and a gesture toward a table by the window where a woman in her seventies was sitting. She wore a heavy sweater and a dark dress. Boulder sat down and introduced himself.

"I have a very unique case," she said with a smile. Boulder detected a warmth about her that did not come across on the telephone. "Someone is sending me

money and I don't know who it is."

"I wish I had that problem," replied Boulder with a grin.

"Seriously, it is a curse when one doesn't know who or why it is being sent."

"I agree," said Boulder. "Tell me about it."

She told him that every Monday since Thanksgiving she had received a letter with a hundred dollar bill and an index card. She also told him that she surmised that it had something to do with the minor collision with the red sports car. Could Boulder find out who was sending the letters?

"It's possible," he said. "Even probable. Why do you want to find out who it is?"

"I'm afraid," she said. "I know what it feels like when someone is stalking someone. Lindsey says that you can find anybody. Would you take my case?"

"Have you ever been stalked?" asked Boulder.

"Well, no."

"Then how do you know how it feels?" asked Boulder, matter-of-factly.

"It was just a figure of speech," she said, embarrassed. "What I meant was that NOW I know how it feels to be stalked. I have this feeling that he is watching me. Would you take my case?"

"I would certainly consider it," he said. "May I see the envelopes?" She reached in her purse and handed him four envelopes.

"How much do you charge to find somebody?"

"My fee is based on how much time I actually spend on the case, plus actual expenses," he said, then quoted her his hourly rate.

She raised her jaw and said, "I had no idea a private detective costs so much."

"There are others who would do it cheaper," he said. "I can give you a list if you would like."

"No, no," she responded quickly. " I want to find this person, and Lindsey said that you are the best. Can you give me your qualifications, if you don't mind?"

"I don't mind at all," he said. "I retired two years ago from the St. Louis Police Department where I was a homicide detective for over ten years. I grew up in Jackson, so I decided to return to Mississippi for my retirement. I opened up my own business, and work out of my residence. I'm strictly a one-man operation, but I choose my cases carefully since I can afford to. Most of my clients are insurance companies, law firms or private individuals. I'll be glad to give you a list of references."

"Lindsey is the only reference I need."

"By the way, how is Lindsey?"

"Fine," she replied. "She works at Lampton's."

"What's Lampton's?" he asked.

"It's a department store on Main Street."

"Good," he said. "I'll stop by and see her. I need to do some Christmas shopping anyway."

They continued talking and both ate too much of an excellent lunch. Boulder asked questions about the col-

lision and about other aspects of her life. Boulder did not say so, but he was fascinated with this case. He felt a challenge brewing. Christmas season was going to be busy for him this year.

"So when can you get started?" she asked.

"First thing tomorrow," he said.

He left her at the Round Table and went to Lampton's where he found Lindsey. They spent a few minutes catching up on her life, then he managed to spend $400 on Christmas presents for his girlfriend.

"Tell me about your girlfriend," said Lindsey.

"Her name is Laura Webster," said Boulder, with a grin. "She's a lawyer with a big law firm in Jackson and she was my high school sweetheart."

"Why don't you marry her?"

"We are doing just fine the way we are. Both of us

are afraid that marriage might spoil things," said Boulder. "How's the kid?"

"He's great," said Lindsey proudly. "Thank goodness I've got Mama to help."

"Good," he said, picking up his shopping bags.

"Can you do me a favor?" she asked.

"Name it."

"Do all you can for Maggie. She's a nice woman. She really is."

"You can count on it," he said with a wink.

He left and drove back to Jackson looking forward to tomorrow. On the way he thought about the case and began planning. The envelopes came from Hattiesburg. He couldn't wait to find out how many Corvettes there were in Hattiesburg.

Chapter 6

The next day Jack Boulder learned through a law enforcement contact that there were four red Corvettes in the Hattiesburg area registered with the State Department of Motor Vehicles. By 6:00 p.m. he had checked into a local motel and was scanning the Hattiesburg telephone directory.

Three of the four Corvettes were registered in men's names, the other in the name of a woman. Boulder sat at the motel room's small desk and laid out three cards in front of him. Each bore a name. He retrieved the local telephone directory, and searched for a residential listing for G.W. Beckwith, one of the names on a card. He found no G.W. Beckwith or any name that began with those initials. Not a good omen, he thought.

He had better luck with the second name on the list. James B. Hillman, attorney at law, showed a business and residential address. The third name, Joe B. Conner, wasn't listed as such, but there was a J. B. Conner. Using a Hattiesburg city map, he located the streets of interest and shaded them with a yellow highlighter pen. He killed time until 8:00 p.m. by watching television and going over various scenarios of what the night might bring. Ms. Carswell's description wasn't too helpful, so he had brought along a 35 millimeter camera and telephoto lens. Hopefully, she would be able to identify a photograph of the man in the red Corvette.

He daydreamed awhile about Corvettes. He had almost bought a new one for himself a year and a half ago when he moved back to Jackson. Instead, he succumbed to nostalgia and purchased a 1968 Chevrolet Camaro in decent shape and then fully restored it with the help of a trusted mechanic. It ended up costing as much to restore the Camaro as to purchase a new 'Vette, but he had not regretted his decision. On several occasions he had been offered more than he had invested in the classic beauty.

Boulder left the motel at eight on the hour and drove to the residence address of the attorney, James B. Hillman. It was located in an upscale subdivision on the west side of town. The house was a Louisiana Plantation cottage style, with a large front porch and four fat, white columns. Lattice-work accented a detached two-car carport connected to the main house by a trellis-covered breezeway. A child's red plastic wagon and beach pail lay in the front yard as if forgotten by a mother collecting her child at the end of play. Resting comfortably in the carport under a yellow ceiling light were a dark green sport utility vehicle and a red Corvette. Both looked less than a year old. Boulder felt a tinge of excitement at finding the car, but quickly realized that a neighborhood street was not a good place to be taking photographs. Boulder departed without attention.

His next stop was the address for J. B. Conner. It turned out to be located in a much lower-class neighborhood, one comprised of small ranch houses and two-bedroom cottages in an area that had seen its better days. The street was lined with old cars, some resting wheel-less on cement blocks. He figured that the street would get better the farther along he drove. He was wrong. It occurred to him that this was not a place for expensive sports cars. Just as the thought left his mind, he saw it—a red Corvette parked in a gravel driveway beside a small frame house with an interior light glowing behind one of the front windows. He stopped and surveyed the scene, formulating a plan.

The next morning Boulder was parked in his Camaro a half block down from Conner's house. His engine was shut off so as not to attract attention. The morning air was crisp and cold and still. A thin layer of frost covered the rooftops, vehicles and yards. From each house a small cloud of steam or smoke rose straight up into the atmosphere. The running motor of a car would produce the same white cloud. So Boulder just sat there—still, watching, sipping a cup of warm coffee.

At 7:15 a.m. the front door of Conner's house opened, then slammed with a bang as a man emerged and walked out to the Corvette. Boulder couldn't see him well enough to manage a photograph or even describe him for that matter. Conner—if that's who he was—got in the Corvette and fired up the engine. A squirt of washer fluid doused the windshield, and wipers swiped away the thin layer of frost in one motion. As the white back-up lights illuminated,

Boulder decided that he didn't like this guy already. At least give the engine a minute's warmup on a morning like this. The Corvette backed out onto the street and pulled away at normal speed. Boulder turned on the Camaro's engine and followed a half block behind. Ten minutes later the Corvette pulled into a mobile home sales lot on U.S. Highway 49 North. Boulder unobtrusively pulled into a parking lot across the road and readied his camera. His specially-equipped, automatic-winding camera took four pictures of Conner by the time he walked into the front door of the sales office.

Boulder placed the camera back down on the seat and drove to Hillman's law office, which was in downtown Hattiesburg across from the courthouse. He positioned himself diagonally across the street from the front door of the office. The time was 7:50 a.m. As if on cue, Hillman arrived on the hour. Boulder readied the camera, wondering which of the five front-door parking places the driver of the Corvette would choose. Probably the one on the right. The car drove into an alley beside the building. Boulder muttered a mild curse under his breath, evaluating options. Less than a minute later Hillman appeared on foot in the alley, wrapped in a beige trench coat and carrying a large black briefcase. Boulder's camera got seven shots of the attorney.

Boulder spent the next hour in an unsuccessful attempt to locate G.W. Beckwith. He then had the film developed at a one-hour photo shop. Finding the prints to be excellent, he got in his car and made the thirty-minute drive to Columbia. Maybe Ms. Carswell would recognize one of these men. Less than an hour later he was sitting in his client's living room.

"That's him. That one right there," said Margaret Carswell, pointing to one of the photos on the coffee table in front of her.

Chapter 7

"Who is he?" asked Maggie Carswell.

They were side-by-side on a sofa in her living room, both leaning forward over the coffee table. Two cups of hot chocolate were steaming beside the photos. Boulder picked up his cup and took a noisy sip, careful not to burn his tongue.

"Probably a man named J. B. Conner," replied Boulder. "But I can't be certain just yet." He pointed his right index finger at the photograph. "All I know is that this person apparently lives at an address for J. B. Conner, and that he drives a red Corvette."

"What do we do now?" she asked.

"That's up to you, Ms. Carswell. If this is indeed Conner, and if he is the one who sent you those letters, then I suppose you would need to talk to the Postal Inspector's Office to determine if a crime has been committed."

"Oh, I know he didn't commit a crime," she said. "You don't have to be so gentle with an old lady. I just want to know why he's doing it. Can you find that out for me?"

"All I know to do is ask him," said Boulder.

"Well, then, you had better go ask him," she said, standing up and signaling the end of the conversation.

He followed her to the front door and then out onto the large front porch. The sun had come out and was warming the day. As he was about to descend the steps, he stopped and turned towards the base of a large pecan tree in the front yard. He stared at the tree.

"What is it?" she asked with concern. Had Boulder spied a stalker?

"Look under that tree," whispered Boulder, still staring, frozen in his tracks like a bird dog that has spotted a quail. "An albino squirrel."

She walked over to the edge of the porch and smiled a knowing smile at Boulder. She clasped her hands and said, "That's what most people think. It's not albino; it's a white squirrel. Governor Hugh White brought them to Columbia many years ago.

"I beg your pardon," he said.

"He went on a trip to some state up north—I believe it was Minnesota—and saw this breed of squirrel that is white. He made sure that a few got to Mississippi. That's why people see white squirrels in Columbia. They are not albino."

"Oh," he said, still processing this information.

"It's obvious you have never heard of Hugh White," she said.

"No."

"Well, let me tell you about him," she said. "No! I'll do better than that. Come on back in."

They went back inside and while he made himself comfortable on the living room sofa, she fetched a book and brought it to him. "Here. Read this."

The book was entitled, "History of Marion County,

Mississippi." He read that Hugh White was Columbia's most favorite son. He was not only Governor of Mississippi, but he started the Balance Agriculture With Industry program, an economic development program since copied by many other states.

White ran a lumber mill and was extremely active in the community. The list of his charitable activities included support of missionaries in Brazil and China, college education for many boys and girls, and large contributions to numerous churches. His business had a written policy of contributing ten percent of all profits to charity. He was elected Governor of Mississippi in 1936 and again in 1952.

During his first term as Governor he originated his famous Balance Agriculture With Industry program, which was actually an outgrowth of the Columbia Plan. Boulder read on with interest.

The Mayor of Columbia was Hugh L. White. Unlike many of the big operators who exploited the long leaf pine forests, White did not pocket the profits and move on when the timber was gone. He cast his lot with the people, and having been drafted by them to serve, he now felt a sense of responsibility for the town which had grown with his holdings. Savings of the lumber mill employees were soon spent. Credit was getting tight; the problem was becoming acute. White put his mind to the task of saving the town. He counseled with several close friends, then called a meeting of leading citizens and explained his plan. The chamber of commerce was reorganized and began to search for an industry. With the help of a Chicago location broker, contact was made with a garment manufacturer who wanted to set up a plant in the South. Under the plan initiated by White and local citizens, a building would be constructed to house the manufacturing operation. The necessary land and building required an expenditure of eighty thousand dollars. In spite of the predictions of local pessimists, the chamber of commerce obtained contributions in this amount with White setting the pattern with a sizable gift. Other well-to-do citizens gave substantial amounts and a large number of small contributors rounded out the total, some paying as little as fifty cents a month. Personal notes were given to be paid by installments. This display of faith was encouraging, but cash was needed. A New Orleans bank advanced the entire amount of the unpaid notes on the signatures of White and forty other citizens on a master note. The building was soon under construction, and when it was completed, the Reliance Manufacturing Company moved in and began operations.

From the beginning the industry was a success. So seven hundred employees were punching the time clock and taking home a weekly pay check. . . .

Soon other communities were showing interest (in the Columbia Plan), and White found himself in great demand as a speaker for chambers of commerce and civic clubs. When he announced that retail sales in

Columbia had increased twenty-six percent while the state as a whole showed a thirty-two percent decline during the same period, newspaper men rushed out to write headlines. The Columbia Plan was reviewed all over the state and the local chamber of commerce received inquiries from a majority of the state's municipalities.

Eventually, White was elected Governor of Mississippi, and his famous BAWI plan became the model for economic development incentives around the country. In the mid-1930's only Michigan surpassed Mississippi in the percentage increase in manufacturing. Within a decade, per capita income had more than doubled.

"This is quite a story," said Boulder, setting the book on the coffee table.

"You bet it is," said Maggie. "And it's because of him we have white squirrels in Columbia. It's also time to end the history lesson so you can go talk to Mr. Conner."

Boulder departed and by mid-afternoon was back in Hattiesburg. During the short drive he considered the alternatives available for finding out why Conner was mailing the letters and money to Margaret Carswell. He decided that the best thing to do was simply catch him in the act of mailing a letter and confront him. Of course, that was easier said than done.

Chapter 8

The Corvette was still parked at the mobile home lot when Boulder arrived at 3:30 p.m. He found an inconspicuous spot in the parking lot across the road, and waited. At 5:40 p.m. Conner emerged from the sales office and drove away in the red Corvette. Boulder pulled out and followed. Darkness was setting in, making it easier for Boulder to stay close without causing suspicion. Conner drove back to the small house, got out and went inside, leaving the driver's door open and the car running. Boulder drove past and parked a half-block away in the same place he had been that morning. Less than two minutes later Conner got back in the car and drove away in the direction from which he had come. Boulder tagged along, wondering where this was going to lead. Conner drove to a nearby post office, parked the car and walked inside. Boulder did the same, being as inconspicuous as possible. Conner walked up to a mail slot and withdrew a white envelope from his jacket. Then he did something most people do before mailing a letter. He looked down at the front of the envelope. That instant's hesitation gave Boulder the split-second he needed. He reached over Conner's shoulder and grabbed his wrist. Not too hard, for he wanted to be able to talk his way out of the situation, but hard enough to turn and see the envelope. When Conner felt the pressure on his wrist he let out a yelp and jumped aside as if he had touched a hot pan. The envelope fell to the floor. Boulder promptly dropped down and retrieved it in a smooth agile motion. Sure enough, it was addressed to Margaret Carswell. He held the envelope between himself and the other man, who now had the look of fear written all over him.

"I believe you dropped something," said Boulder.

Conner stood there, frozen in panic. All he could say was "Hey man, please! Hey man, please!" with a gasp.

Boulder produced a small cellular telephone and held it up in front of Conner's face. "I've already dialed in the number of the police department. All I have to do is push the 'send' button and we will have company in no time."

"No. Don't do that," said Conner breathlessly. "I can explain."

"Make it quick."

"It's a long story," Conner replied. Suddenly he was remarkably calm. "Why don't you let me buy you a drink and give you all the details. You will understand then."

"You'd better start talking now or this button is going to be pushed," said Boulder firmly.

Just then the plate glass front door to the post office lobby swung open and a middle-aged woman in business attire walked in carrying an armload of large, brown envelopes. When she saw the two men in the lobby, one holding up both hands with something in each, she stopped and backed out the door.

"Really. I promise," said Conner. "There is a good explanation. Look, here's my wallet."

He handed Boulder a brown leather billfold from his pocket. Boulder peered inside. There was a hundred dollar bill and several credit cards. There was also a Mississippi driver's license. Boulder removed the driver's license and gave the wallet back to Conner.

"I'll follow you," he said.

Chapter 9

J. B. Conner, who was apparently a mobile home salesman, drove to a smokey franchise steak house on Hardy Street, while Jack Boulder, in his detective mode, stayed less than two car lengths behind. They were escorted to a booth against the back wall by a plump uniformed hostess. Boulder's eyes burned at the mixture of haze caused by the grilling of steaks and the puffing of cigarettes from the smoking side of the restaurant. The smoke did not discriminate. It rose above the wagon-wheel light fixtures and then coated the wood-plank walls and red-checked tablecloths with a subtle layer of yellow nicotine.

A female server in her mid-twenties approached their booth, laid two menus on the table, and between chomps on her cinnamon-flavored chewing gum said, "Hi, J. B. Are y'all gonna have the buffet tonight?"

"No, darlin'," said Conner in an accent that sounded a little more country than before. "We'll look at the menu for a minute, then decide."

Boulder hadn't noticed it before, but he saw that Conner was wearing a dress denim western suit and red polyester shirt with imitation pearl buttons. He actually wore it well. Conner was a lanky, sandy-haired character who didn't quite reach six feet in height. He had an oversized, pointed nose and long, bony fingers. All he needed was a nylon scarf around his neck and he could have been a sidekick to a singing cowboy.

When the server returned, they each ordered a steak and all the trimmings. Conner then began his story.

"My daddy and mama were so poor that nowadays they would be considered migrant workers. That's really what they were. They went from one end of the state to the other working whatever crop was in season. They finally settled down in Marion County where they met John Carswell of Columbia. He was one of the richest men in those parts forty years ago. He had a lot of land. He was all business. Someone said that he had ice water running through his veins. But his wife had a heart. The best heart in Mississippi was that of Maggie Carswell. John Carswell let my daddy and mama live on forty acres of land, just north of Columbia, because his wife wouldn't let him kick us off. Daddy paid rent when he could; sometimes we paid in vegetables or whatever was growing in the field."

The server returned with their meals. Conner shook up a bottle of A-1 Steak Sauce and covered his T-bone with it. He cut his steak into bite-sized pieces then stabbed one of the morsels with the fork in his left hand and placed it in his mouth. He chewed and talked at the same time.

"Many were the days that Mrs. Carswell would bring us things like clothes, school supplies and such. I remember the first day of school in the sixth grade. We kids were supposed to bring all these notebooks and a certain kind of paper, not to mention the pens and pencils. I didn't have any of it and didn't know how I was going to get it. It was a bad year. I knew it was a bad year because we ate a lot of biscuits and beans. We had cheese sometimes too. We used to go into town and get commodities. Have you ever heard of commodities, Mr. Boulder?"

"Can't say that I have."

"It's the food handouts that the government used to give before they started giving food stamps. Those were the days when you got actual food. Anyway, as I was saying, I came home crying from school because I didn't have the supplies and the other kids were laughing at me because of it. They called me 'poor white trash.' That's a terrible thing to be called. Later that night—right after sundown—Mrs. Carswell came to our house. She had a big brown paper bag from one of the stores in downtown Columbia. She left it with my mother and told her to give it to me. Inside that brown paper bag were supplies to last me all year. There were Blue Horse notebooks and pencils galore. There was even a pencil sharpener. There was also an envelope with three one dollar bills inside it. I don't know how she heard about my day at school, but she responded in a kind way. I've never forgotten that."

"Is that why you are sending her money?" asked Boulder. "To pay her back."

"No. But let me finish," said Conner, sipping iced tea from a large red plastic glass. "When I was eighteen, we hit hard times again. We couldn't pay any rent with money or food. My father had a long talk with Mr. Carswell, who said that he was going to have to ask us to leave. The next day, Mrs. Carswell came out and told my mother to forget what her husband said. She said that we could stay even if we were behind on our rent. We stayed another year then moved away, owing a whole year's rent. Things got tough after that. Daddy died in a hunting accident and mother raised us herself—that is, my sister and me. I did a little figuring on how much we owed in back rent with interest. Yes, it's a tidy sum."

"What are you getting at?" asked Boulder.

"I hear through the grapevine that Mrs. Carswell has come upon some bad times since her husband died a few years back. All I was doing was trying to help her like she helped us. Nothing wrong with that, is it?"

"Why don't you let her know where the money is coming from?"

"You know the answer to that," said Conner. "She wouldn't take it. If it stays anonymous, then she will have to take it. Besides, that's the way somebody ought to give—anonymously."

"How long did you plan on sending her money?"

"As long as she needs it."

"And just where do you get your money?" asked Boulder.

"I make good money selling mobile homes. Did you know that manufactured housing is growing faster than stick-built housing?"

"Had no idea."

"Anyway, there's just me, and my expenses are not that much," said Conner.

Boulder wiped his lips with a napkin and laid it on the table in front of him. He leaned forward and said, "Ms. Carswell hired me to find out who was sending her the letters. I have a duty to report to her who you are."

"I can understand that, but I wish you wouldn't do it. I just want to help her a little like she helped my mother."

"I'll think about it," said Boulder.

The server reappeared and removed their plates. They sat there for a moment in silence—then Boulder asked, "Why were you in Columbia that day of the collision?"

"Just looking around. I wanted to see her house." He fidgeted with his shirt sleeves, pulling them down on his wrists.

"Was it really an accident?" asked Boulder, his eyes burrowing into those of Conner.

"Maybe I wanted it to happen. Maybe I didn't. I can't say as I really know." He reached back in his wallet and pulled out a hundred dollar bill, then motioned the server to bring the bill. "Allow me to treat tonight."

"You never told me what happened in your life from the time you were eighteen," said Boulder.

"Nothing unusual," said Conner. "Had enough of education and formal learning by the time I finished high school. Joined the Air Force. Been selling things since I got out. Mostly cars. Now I sell mobile homes. I do all right."

"How old are you?"

"Be fifty-four on my next birthday."

"Married?" asked Boulder, knowing the response.

"Just once. It didn't last though. No kids, thank goodness."

"Ever been arrested?"

"What kind of question is that?"

"It's my job to ask questions and find out things," said Boulder. "Especially of someone who is sending my client anonymous letters."

"No. I've never been arrested."

"Just asking," replied Boulder with a smirk.

"What are you going to do now?" asked Conner.

"Say good night, and thanks for the meal," said Boulder as he stood up.

Boulder left the restaurant and drove away in his Camaro. Conner remained seated in the booth. The server reappeared.

"Hey, Patty," said Conner with a grin. "Why don't you and me go find someplace to get crazy after you get off work tonight?"

She winked and said, "Pick me up at eleven."

Chapter 10

John Carswell, Jr., attorney at law, was not in the best of moods. Business was slow, as it always was in the winter. He stared out of his office toward the courthouse and thought about his situation. His income this past year was ten percent less than the year before, but his expenses were much greater. And they would get worse. With a daughter in college and a son about to graduate high school, it could get financially devastating before too much longer. He needed a big case.

He toyed with the idea of putting his country club membership in suspension, but that would only alert his contemporaries that he was having financial difficulties. He dreaded having to ask his wife to reduce her budget, for he knew that she would belittle him. To all outside appearances his marriage was perfect. Even his wife would probably rate it close to perfect. To John Carswell, it was a burden to endure. His wife was a spoiled nag who used him as an income stream to finance her chosen lifestyle. He did not look forward to the coming evening. She had spent the better part of the afternoon test-driving new sport utility vehicles. The kind that cost as much as the finest luxury cars. "My Lincoln is so out-of-style," she had told him the day before.

The telephone intercom rang and his secretary announced that his sister was here to see him. "Tell her to have a seat in the reception room and that I'll be right out."

Joanna Carswell, his sister, was ten years younger and taught at Columbia High School. She was attractive and fit in a rugged sort of way. Once she had modeled a brand of athletic wear for a New Orleans department store in a series of newspaper advertisements. She may have been in her mid-forties, but she had the body of a thirty-year old. During summer vacations she traveled to exotic locations in search of adventure. She had hiked most of the Appalachian Trail, collected butterflies in Central America, canoed the rapids of several wild rivers in Mexico, and photographed mountain sheep in Tibet. She was a popular instructor at school and had won several teaching awards. She was once selected as a STAR teacher, considered by many as the ultimate recognition for a high school teacher in Mississippi. She had never been married and had never dated a man who lived in Columbia. She was always out of town on weekends, leading to much speculation by those who fulfill their yearning souls with gossip.

Like her brother, John, she had received $100,000 in cash on the occasion of the death of their father, ten years ago. Unknown to any family members, John Carswell, Sr. had set up two accounts at Trustmark National Bank in their names, with instructions to the bank to inform them of it upon his death. Joanna had invested hers in the stock market and it had grown considerably. John had placed his in a savings account and drawn on it to maintain his family's lifestyle. He had exhausted it two years ago and was now in debt to his sister to the tune of $35,000.

"Good morning, Joanna," said John with a forced smile. "Come in." They went inside his large, high-ceilinged, dark-paneled office and took seats at a conference table on the opposite side of the room from his desk. "Guess you know why I asked you to come by."

"Same as always," she replied, exhaling loudly. "You need money."

"Do you want to know what I want to use it for?"

"Nope. Have you talked to Mother lately?" asked Joanna.

"I call her at least twice a week."

"How is she doing?"

"Just fine, I guess," said John. "Why?"

"Has she gotten over Thanksgiving?"

"What do you mean?"

"Thanksgiving," snarled Joanna. "You know. It's a holiday that comes around every November. Pilgrims. Turkeys." She stood up and walked over to the window. "It's the time when families are supposed to be together. Not split up like our family was this year. So what I mean is, has mother gotten over the fact that she was snubbed for Thanksgiving this year by her two children?"

"Oh, cut it out," retorted John. "We invited her to our house. She wasn't snubbed."

"And she invited all of us to HER house!"

"Don't get so upset," he said. "You had to be on a school trip to New York with the high school band."

"But you could have been there for her, John," she pleaded. "If you would stand up to your wife once and a while, you wouldn't be in these situations!"

John realized that the conversation was turning into an argument. He needed to calm down. She was right. Sharon had not wanted to go to his mother's house for Thanksgiving. And he didn't even argue.

"You're right, as usual," he said. "Now can I borrow some money for a few weeks? I've got a case that will be settled any day."

She shook her head slowly back and forth. "John. John. How much?"

"Twenty-five thousand," he said in a low voice.

"Are you getting into financial trouble? Are you a compulsive gambler?"

"No. It's just a cash flow problem. That's all," he said.

She knew that it was hopeless to attempt to persuade him to change his ways. She said she would make arrangements to transfer the funds and that they would be in his business checking account by noon tomorrow. He thanked her profusely, then hugged her.

"I don't know what I would do without you," he said.

"I know," she replied with a tone of resignation.

As she walked out the door, he picked up the telephone to call home. Sharon answered on the first ring. She immediately told him that she had found the most gorgeous new Explorer at Mike Smith Motors. And they would take her Lincoln in on trade.

"That's wonderful, dear," he said and hung up the telephone. He turned and kicked a hole in the side of his desk.

Chapter 11

Maggie Carson was up and dressed in time to watch "The Today Show," which she never missed. On this day there was a feature story on studies that showed that having a pet made people live longer. Even with two children there had never been a pet in the Carswell household. Her husband John did not want one in the yard either because he said that a dog required a fence, and a fence detracted from the appearance of the house and yard. So the Carswells never had a pet. Maybe it was time to change that, she thought. It would be a good day to find a pet. She would call Lindsey, who would know about such things. A lap dog would be nice.

At 9:30 a.m. the front doorbell rang as expected. There on the porch was Jack Boulder, who had called yesterday and said that he had found the letter writer. Maggie's heart was beating fast as she welcomed him inside.

"So you found him?" she said, gesturing him to the living room sofa.

"That I did," said Boulder with a touch of pride.

"Can I get you some hot chocolate first?"

"No, thank you."

"I'm so nervous," she said, sitting down. "Tell me about him."

Boulder opened a file jacket and said, "His name is

James B. Conner. He goes by the initials, J.B. He's a mobile home salesman in Hattiesburg and he says that he is doing this because he thinks you need money." Boulder went on to tell every detail of what Conner had said in the restaurant.

"Isn't that the most unusual thing?"

"Yes, it is," said Boulder. "He requested that I not reveal his name to you, but I told him that's what you hired me for. Do you remember him or his family?"

"Let me see," she said, touching her right index finger to her chin. "My husband had quite a few families who lived on our property. I'm afraid that I really don't recall a family by the name of Conner."

"I don't think he will be sending you any more letters," said Boulder.

She scrunched her face, seeming pained at this news. "I suppose not." She lowered her head, deep in thought. After a few seconds she looked up at Boulder and said almost triumphantly, "I want to meet him."

"What?"

"I want to meet him," said Maggie. "Or meet him again, I should say."

"I don't think that's such a good idea, Ms. Carswell. There is still a lot about J.B. Conner that we don't know."

"You're right," she said with her chin up. "So you keep checking while I meet him."

"Really, it's . . . " began Boulder.

"No really about it." She was energized. "Invite him

to come to dinner tonight."

"I wouldn't recommend inviting him into your home," said Boulder. "Not just yet."

"What's wrong with my home? Call him and ask him to come to dinner tonight. I want you to stay here too if it makes you feel better. I'll have it no other way. The telephone is in the hallway," she said, pointing a finger in that direction.

Boulder did as instructed, calling directory assistance first to get the phone number of Conner's employer. When Conner heard the invitation, he accepted immediately and said that he would be there for dinner at 7:00 p.m. As Boulder hung up the telephone, he realized that Conner did not ask for the address.

At ten minutes before the appointed time, Maggie Carswell and Jack Boulder heard the distinctive sound of Corvette exhaust pipes. Within seconds the doorbell sounded, and Maggie opened the door to J.B. Conner. He was dressed in a royal blue western suit and holding a batch of fresh flowers in his left hand.

"Oh, how pretty," said Maggie, gleefully accepting the flowers. "Come in while I put them in a vase. You know Mr. Boulder, I believe."

"Yes, ma'am," said Conner as he stepped across the threshold, touching his right hand to his forehead in a mock salute.

After an appropriate amount of small talk, Maggie announced that dinner was served. They moved to the adjoining dining room, where the flowers now graced the center of the table. They feasted on beef stroganoff, salad and lemon ice box pie. "I made the pie, but got the rest from a caterer here in town. She's one of the best around. If you ever need a caterer, just look across the alley behind the Back Door Cafe." The dinner was truly an enjoyable occasion. Boulder was somewhat taken back at how amicable Maggie and J.B. were to each other. After dinner, Maggie served coffee, whereupon the conversation became more serious.

"Ms. Carswell," said Conner. "I apologize to you for causing you any distress. I certainly did not intend to do that. As a matter of fact, I wanted to do just the opposite. I guess Mr. Boulder here told you what I had heard about your financial condition."

"Yes, he did," she replied. "And I want you to know that nothing could be further from the truth."

"Well, I'm happy to hear that. But still, I think it only fair that I pay Mr. Boulder's fee. After all, I was the cause of that expense."

"I'll hear of no such thing."

They sat and talked for almost an hour. Conner recounted his story about growing up and other tales of how people in Columbia helped his family. Boulder thought it all a little too corny. But Maggie Carswell loved every word of it. At 8:45 p.m. Maggie went to the kitchen and asked Boulder to join her.

"I think it's time you left, Mr. Boulder," she said. "I would like to spend some time alone with Mr. Conner. He's a very refreshing person, don't you think?" she asked with almost a school-girl grin.

"I don't think . . . "

"I know. You don't think it's a good idea," she said interrupting him.

"Look . . . "

"Good night, Mr. Boulder," she said emphatically, placing her hands on his chest and gently pushing him back. "I can take care of myself." And with a wave, she almost sang, "Don't forget to send me your bill."

Boulder realized there would be no use in arguing. She was apparently infatuated with this cowboy. Very well. She was a grown woman and she could do as she pleased. He had done his job and he would send her a bill as requested. People had the right to be foolish, and far be it from him to tell someone how to run her life. Boulder feigned the need to get back to Jackson and left them alone in the living room. He drove back to Jackson, arriving at his downtown condominium after 11:00 p.m. The blinking red light on his answering machine caught his attention as he walked in the door. He punched a button and listened to the only message.

"Hey, Jack," said the male voice. "This is you-know-who. I got the background check on Joe B. Conner, white male, age fifty-four. He's got three arrests and one conviction for false pretenses going back about ten years ago. Also, he served time in the county jail on the Gulf Coast for possession of stolen property. No outstanding wants or warrants. Call me if you need anything else."

Chapter 12

Lindsey Plummer's phone rang just as she was heading out the door for work. She debated whether to answer it, but after six rings she figured that someone was trying really hard to get her. She was right.

"Hi Lindsey, this is Jack Boulder in Jackson."

"Of course! It's good to hear from you. How's the case with Miz Maggie going?"

"That's what I called you about," said Boulder. "I found the guy who was sending her the letters and she wanted to meet him. Last night I left them alone at her house—at her insistence, of course. Is she supposed to be going to work today? I didn't get an answer when I called her home number just now."

"She's probably on the way to the store right now," said Lindsey. "Want me to have her call you?"

"Please do."

They said fond good-byes and Lindsey drove to the Lampton Company, barely making it on time by 9:00 a.m. She clocked in and began getting ready for the day, knowing that it would be one of the busiest days of the year. She was getting tired just thinking about it. She went to Hill Hardware and asked every employee about Maggie. No one had seen her yet. It was not like Maggie to be late. She went back to Lampton's to a private office in the back part of the store and dialed Maggie's home telephone number. There was no answer after eight rings. That meant she was on the way to the store.

Thirty minutes later there was still no sign of Maggie at Hill Hardware. Lindsey called one more time with the same results. She began to worry, then remembered that Jack Boulder had asked her to call him back. She made a collect call, and he instantly accepted the charges.

"She's not at the store," said Lindsey. "And there's no answer at her home number."

"I know," said Boulder. "I've been trying it myself. I know this is asking a lot, but could you go over to her house and check around?"

"I'm on my way," she said. "Call you back shortly."

Lindsey told her supervisor where she was going, then drove directly to Maggie's house. As she pulled in the driveway, she noticed Maggie's car in the garage. She went to the front door and rang the doorbell. There was no response. She knocked hard on the door. Still no sign of life inside. She walked around the side of the house to the back door and banged on it, calling Maggie's name. Finally she went to Maggie's bedroom and peered inside through a small opening where the shade had not been pulled all the way down. What she saw made her blood run cold. There was a hump in Maggie's bed, like someone sleeping under covers. But there was no movement. Lindsey banged on the windows. Was she looking at a corpse?

Lindsey did the only thing that she knew to do. She

dashed to the house next door and told the neighbor to call the police and an ambulance. "I think something has happened to Miz Maggie!"

Although it seemed like a half hour to Lindsey, the police arrived in less than four minutes. She told the two officers that Maggie didn't show up for work and that when she came to check on her, she was in her bed not moving. She took them to the bedroom window and showed them. They hustled to the back door and kicked it open. Lindsey followed them inside, tears now forming in her eyes. The three of them rushed to the bedroom. One of the officers reached out and touched the still form on the bed. As he did so, Maggie Carswell jerked over on her back and screamed.

The first officer jumped back, ramming the second officer in the chest. Reaching out to brace himself, the second officer struck a lamp, causing it to crash to the floor. The officer fell to the floor. Lindsey let out a loud scream, then brought her hands up over her mouth. And then there was silence.

Maggie, who was now sitting up in her bed, clutching the covers up to her chin, surveyed the scene in her bedroom, attempting to comprehend what was happening. The two officers just looked at each other. Lindsey was staring at Maggie as if she had seen a ghost.

"Are you all right?" asked Lindsey.

"Of course," she said cautiously. "Why are all of you in my room?"

"When you didn't show up for work, I got worried. Then you didn't answer the door."

"Oh, my goodness" said Maggie. "I guess I overslept." She looked at the officers, both of whom were now standing at the foot of the bed, and said, "I'm so sorry you had to be bothered."

"No problem, ma'am," shrugged one. "It's part of our job. We will be leaving now if you are okay?"

"I'm fine, thank you."

They departed out the back door. Lindsey sat down in a chair beside the bed.

"What time did you go to bed last night?" asked Lindsey.

"Well, it was—let's see—after the ten o'clock news, I remember that." She looked around. "I'm not sure that I remember. We were having such a good time."

"You and . . ."

"J.B.," said Maggie, completing the sentence.

"J.B.?" repeated Lindsey.

"Yes. He's the man who was sending me the letters. He thought I was broke and needed money. Can you imagine that? He's the nicest man. I can't remember when I've felt so young. Let me get up and make us some hot chocolate and I'll tell you all about him." There was an enthusiasm in her voice that Lindsey had not heard before.

"I've got to get back to work," said Lindsey.

"Oh, yes. Work. Tell them I'll be a little late today. I have a few things to do."

"You seem awfully happy, Ms. Maggie."

"Child, I have never been happier in my life," she said with a wide grin.

Chapter 13

Students of architecture still study Columbia High School, which was opened in 1937 during a period of growing expenditures in the public school infrastructure in Mississippi. It is a large two-story building, designed by renowned architects Hays Town and James Overstreet.

On the second floor of the school, Joanna Carswell was giving her students their daily quiz when she received a note to call her brother as soon as possible. She thought that to be highly unusual, as he knew what time classes were over for the day. She went through the motions of instruction with her brother's note in the back of her mind. Please don't let him want to borrow more money. It was possible that he really did have a gambling problem and had gotten in over his head. Boy, that would be something that would shake up Columbia. A prominent lawyer declaring bankruptcy. Finally the end of class arrived. She went to the teacher's lounge and dialed his number.

"You are not going to believe what is happening," he said when he got on the telephone.

"What?"

"The police were called this morning to Mother's house after she didn't show up for work," he said, flaunting the fact that he knew something that she did not know.

"And?"

"Turns out she just overslept. But I talked to one of her neighbors who told me that a red Corvette was parked in her driveway until around midnight."

"Who could that have been?" asked Joanna.

"I don't know yet, but I'm working on it," he said.

Joanna could not mask her frustration. "Well, why don't you just call Mother and ask her? Why do you have to be so damn secretive about everything?"

There was silence.

"Are you still there?"

"Of course," he answered. "Well, I've got to go. I just thought you would want to know."

Sometimes he drove her crazy with his back door approaches. When they were kids playing in City Park, he was always sneaking up on other kids. She decided to take matters into her own hands without waiting on her brother. She dialed her mother's telephone number. Maggie Carswell answered on the third ring.

"Mother, what was all the commotion over there this morning? I heard that the police paid you a visit," said Joanna.

"Oh, yes," said Maggie. "It was so terribly embarrassing and exciting all at the same time. I just overslept, that's all."

"What made you oversleep? That's not like you."

"If you must know, I had a visitor who stayed late last night," said Maggie.

"Really. And who might this be?" asked Joanna.

"A gentleman that I met."

Joanna was speechless. Part of her wanted her mother to find a male friend. But another part of her wanted to preserve the memory of her mother and father as a couple. All she could say was, "A gentleman?"

"That's right. He's very nice. Maybe you can meet him soon. He's coming back over tonight and we're going out to dinner."

"Oh," she said, stunned. "Well, keep me up to date on your . . . uh . . . date."

"Ha, ha," she laughed. "That's cute. Talk to you later."

Joanna realized that she was still standing. She sat down and digested what she had just heard. Mother might be getting a boyfriend. How interesting. How exciting. That's not such a bad thing. Way to go, Mom! She immediately called her brother and told him the news.

"Oh, my God," said John, Jr. "That's not good."

"Why not?"

"Well, it's just not," he stammered. "I'm not sure why. It's just not."

"Get over it, John," she intoned. "It's time for Mother to start living. It's been ten years since Daddy died. She's entitled to it. Besides, what could be wrong with that?"

"Nothing," he said. "Nothing."

He hung up the phone and stared out the window at the courthouse. Nothing, indeed. He reached up to the bookcase on his wall and withdrew a volume of the Mississippi Code. Mother didn't have a will. According to the law of descent and distribution in Mississippi, her estate would go to her heirs, which in this case were John and Joanna. The estate was worth well over a million dollars. If she married, then her husband would get a child's share, meaning that the estate would be divided into three parts instead of two. He would be out over a quarter million dollars. Either his mother would have to make a will, preferably one splitting the estate evenly between himself and his sister, or this fellow she was seeing would have to go. He leaned back in his chair and began formulating a plan.

Chapter 14

When Lindsey returned to the store, she called Jack Boulder collect and reported that Maggie had only overslept due to being up late last night with a gentleman guest. Boulder was concerned.

"I don't like it, Lindsey," he said. "I've discovered some additional information about J.B. Conner that I believe Maggie should know about."

"She's at home right now if you want to give her a call," said Lindsey.

"I think I'd rather tell her in person. I'm on my way to Columbia."

Two hours later, Jack Boulder drove his 1968 Camaro down Main Street. It occurred to him that this little three blocks of Main Street was just like a shopping mall. No, it was just the opposite. The shopping malls were just like this little Main Street. What the malls had attempted to recreate was right here in real life. He surveyed the storefronts as he drove by. There was Citizens Bank, the State Farm Insurance agent, J.C. Penney, Merle Norman, G&S Rentals, Berean Bookstore, the Carousel Consignment Shop, Heritage Jewelry, and Cook & Fortenberry Drug Store. The courthouse stood majestically at the end of the street like the throne of a king in the hall of a castle.

Boulder turned left off Main Street and two blocks later pulled up in front of Maggie's house. There were two white squirrels in her front yard this morning. They scampered up a large tree when he opened his car door. He rang the doorbell, but got no answer. He walked over to the side of the porch and peered in back at an empty garage. Maggie must be gone. He got back in his car and drove back to Main Street, where he parked in front of Berlon's Friendly Department Store. He got out and walked to the end of the block to the Lampton Company, where he found Lindsey working behind a register in the gift department. She greeted him with a smile.

"She's not home," Boulder announced. "I'll wait around downtown until she returns."

"The Back Door is open if you want some coffee," she said.

A puzzled look came upon his face and he peered over his shoulder at the rear of the store. "Beg your par-

don," he said.

"Oh, I'm sorry," she said with a laugh. "The Back Door Cafe is located that way." She was pointing. "It's inside the store, but the main entrance to the cafe is from the back door of the department store."

"I think I understand," he said with a smile.

"How about getting us a table," she said. "I'll take my break in a few minutes and meet you there."

He strolled to the back of the store and, sure enough, found a cafe. There was a counter in front of a small commercial kitchen, and tables and booths in a cozy room. Through a large archway was another set of tables conveniently placed in the gift section of the department store. He guessed the place could seat fifty customers at one time. He ordered a cup of coffee and took a seat in the room with the gifts. Three women in their early sixties sat at one table. Each wore a dress and was leaning forward intently, listening to one of their own in animated conversation. In the corner table sat a distinguished-looking older gentleman who sipped slowly on his mug of coffee. He had on a blue shirt and a gray, sleeveless cardigan sweater, which blended well with his head of full, silver hair and matching handlebar mustache. His blue eyes caught Boulder and he nodded a greeting.

Boulder sat down one table over from the man, began sipping his coffee, and studied the room. The ceilings were high and dark. Ten minutes later Lindsey bounced in and sat down at his table. She had a cola in a large glass with a plastic straw growing from its center.

"You sounded serious on the telephone," she said. "I take it you don't approve of Mr. J.B. Conner."

"You can say that again. He's a con man, Lindsey," said Boulder seriously. "He has a record for this sort of thing."

"Oh, my goodness," said Lindsey breathlessly. "We've got to do something."

"Excuse me. I couldn't help but overhear your conversation." It was the man with the silver hair, now leaning forward toward their table. "May I?" he said, gesturing toward a vacant chair at their table. Lindsey and Boulder looked at each other, not really knowing how to react. "Thank you," he said as though he had been invited. He got up and sat down at their table. "I'm curious as to why you're interested in J.B. Conner."

"Sir," said Boulder through tight lips, "is there something we can do for you?"

"Oh no. Nothing at all," he said peevishly. "But there is something I might be able to do for you." He raised his chin. "I've known Joey Conner a long time." He took a sip from his mug and smiled pleasantly. If the man had been a cat, there would be little yellow feathers on his lips.

Boulder and Lindsey looked at each other searching for guidance, then Boulder spoke. "Why don't you tell us about him then?"

"Why don't you tell me why you want to know?" said the man. He was enjoying the game because only he knew the rules.

Lindsey took charge. "Do you know Mrs. Margaret Carswell?" she asked purposefully.

"Of course," he said. "I've known Maggie all my life."

"We're afraid she is being taken advantage of," said Lindsey.

"By Joey Conner?" asked the man, raising one eyebrow.

"Perhaps," said Lindsey.

"There is no perhaps, young lady," the man said. "He's been waiting thirty years to take advantage of anybody associated with John Carswell."

Chapter 15

The comment unsettled Lindsey. She moved back in her chair and crossed her arms as if she had a chill.

"Please explain," said Boulder.

"I'm Ledbetter Moss," he said. Before he could continue, Lindsey jumped in.

"Moss Realty," said Lindsey.

"That's correct."

"Then you're my landlord," she said. She looked at Boulder and said, "I live in one of his apartments. He's the biggest real estate man in Marion County." There was a touch of pride in her voice as if being at the same table with him was something to be desired.

"You're too kind," said Moss. "By the way, is everything satisfactory at your apartment? All the heating equipment work properly? Plumbing working okay?"

"Yes."

"Good," he continued.

"I'm Lindsey Plummer and this is Jack Boulder. He's a private detective." Boulder blushed at the remark. He wished she hadn't said it. Lindsey realized her mistake, but could only lower her head. Boulder stuck out his hand and shook Ledbetter's.

"As I was about to say, I am in the real estate business and have been since they started making real estate." He paused for effect. Lindsey chuckled; Boulder sat stone-faced. "In the past I had occasion to do quite a bit of business with John Carswell. He was an interesting man, a real leader in our community. One of the things he did that most people don't know about is make it possible for many people who could not otherwise afford it to own their own home."

"How did he do that?" asked Lindsey.

"He owned a lot of land. Thousands of acres. One of the things he would do is allow certain poor families to live on his land for just a small amount of rent. Also, he was fond of selling land by using a contract for deed."

"What's that?" asked Boulder.

"Well, in a normal real estate transaction, the seller gives the buyer a deed and then the buyer gives a deed of trust to the lender's trustee. If the buyer defaults on the loan payments, the lender forecloses and the buyer loses the property. The property is then sold on the courthouse steps and if the price doesn't bring enough to cover the remaining balance on the mortgage, then there is a judgement recorded against the buyer for the difference. But in a contract for deed situation, the buyer enters into a contract with the seller that says that the seller will give the buyer a deed ONLY after the property has been paid for."

"Why would anyone want to buy real estate that way?" asked Boulder.

"Someone who cannot get financing has no choice. If you are poor and want to own your own place then you have to either rent, and get no ownership equity built up, or sign a contract for deed. When you finally pay off the contract, it's yours."

"Wouldn't that take a lot of years?" asked Boulder.

"Yes," said Moss. "That is a problem with that method. However, it's better than nothing. Anyway, Joey Conner's father signed a contract for deed to buy the land and small house they were renting from Carswell. I think it was about forty acres. Conner's father worked hard, but was always behind on his payment. Every once and a while he would get some extra cash and pay more. The family lived there about eighteen years and had just about paid for the property. The reason I know it was eighteen years is that they moved in and Joey was born six months later. I think Carswell sympathized with them because the wife was pregnant. Anyway, right after Joey turned eighteen, his father fell behind four or five months in his payment and Carswell told him that he was in default of the contract and to get off the land."

"So, he had to move after paying all those payments?" asked Lindsey. "That's terrible!"

"The father was going to go quietly, but his son, Joey, wasn't going to let Carswell do that to the family. There was a big fight on the front porch of the little house. Joey went after John Carswell and gave him a black eye. To make matters worse, John Carswell sold the property to someone else the very next week for cash. When Joey found out about that, he assumed that the Conners had been forced off the land because

Carswell had a cash buyer. Of course, I don't think Joey really knew that his father was behind on the rent. Anyway, Joey swore that he would get even with Carswell one day even if it took the rest of his life. That's what he said all right. He took it pretty hard. The family moved away after that, but I knew Joey wouldn't forget it."

"How do you know all this, Mr. Moss?" asked Boulder.

"I was with Mr. Carswell that day. He asked me to go with him as a witness that he was giving them their eviction notice."

"So they had paid for eighteen years and got kicked off their land when they only had a few months left?" asked Boulder.

"That's one way of looking at it."

There was a quiet around the table as each person processed this information. Lindsey finally stirred her soft drink. Boulder was the first to speak.

"Was what Carswell did legal?"

"Oh, yes. He was definitely within his legal rights. He gave Conner a lot of chances to make his payments."

"When was the last time you saw Joey Conner?" asked Boulder.

"That was the last time and that was over thirty years ago. But I could tell, Mr. Boulder. This was something that he was not going to forget. The last words I heard him say were that no matter how long it took, Carswell was going pay for what he did."

Chapter 16

After the conversation with Ledbetter Moss, Lindsey went back to work while Boulder began the search for Maggie Carswell. According to Lindsey, Maggie often went to church during the week and did volunteer work. Boulder's first stop was the United Methodist Church, which was located—where else?—on Church Street. Inside he found the pastor's secretary and asked if Margaret Carswell had been in today.

"No," said the secretary. "We haven't seen her today. She usually comes in to help mail out the church bulletin. She usually calls if she can't be here. Is something wrong?"

"I'm not sure," said Boulder. "If she comes in, would you have her call Lindsey. She will understand."

Boulder got back in his Camaro and just cruised around the downtown area for several minutes. After not seeing any evidence of her, he decided that it was time to go to Hattiesburg and have a man-to-man talk with Conner. He drove west on U.S. 98 and soon was pulling into the parking lot of the mobile home dealer where Conner worked. He walked in and was met by a burly middle-aged man with a short pony tail and shoulders that looked like he spent all his free time on the professional wrestling match circuit. Boulder introduced himself and asked to see Conner.

"Sorry, he's not here," said the big guy. "Can someone else help you?"

"Do you know how I can reach him? It's sort of urgent."

"Don't know. He didn't show up for work today. What's this about?"

"Is that unusual?" asked Boulder.

"What?"

"That he didn't show up for work," said Boulder.

"Yea. I guess it is."

"Did you call his home? It's almost noon."

"Look, man. I'm the sales manager here, not the babysitter. Our salesmen don't show up, that's not my business. He works on commission. Hey, he could be out working in the field right now."

"Sure," said Boulder, now agitated. "And I'm commander of the South Pole National Guard." He turned and started to walk out. The sales manager was not going to let him have the last word.

"Hey, buddy," said the brawny man. "When you find J.B., tell him he's fired!"

Boulder quickly got in his car and drove to Conner's residence. As expected, it was locked up tight, with no sign of anyone at home. He returned to Columbia just before lunch and went straight to the Lampton Company, where Lindsey was just about to take her lunch break. He told her about his visits to the church and to Hattiesburg.

"What do you think we should do now?" asked Lindsey, with a pained look on her face. "Shouldn't we file a missing person's report with the police?"

"We don't have enough evidence to suspect foul play, I'm afraid."

"We may not have enough to suspect foul play in St. Louis, but in Columbia, our police department is a little different," she said. "Besides, the dispatcher has been trying to get a date with me for two weeks."

He followed her out the door and they walked around the corner and down 2nd Street, past the City Barber Shop to the Columbia Police Department. The desk sergeant recognized her as soon as she entered the front door.

"Hi, Lindsey," the uniformed officer said.

"Hi, Bob. Is Elton on duty today?"

"He went to get a haircut. Should be back any minute." The front door opened and he looked over Lindsey's shoulder. "Speak of the devil. There he is now."

Walking in the front door was Elton Rhodes, a 6-foot, 4-inch man of twenty-one years of age who looked like he did bodybuilding in his spare time. He wore a gray khaki uniform instead of the dark blue outfits worn be the police officers. Rhodes planned to be wearing a police uniform within six months. He would finish a major in Police Administration this semester, and had already been hired, contingent on his getting the degree. As he entered, Rhodes saw Lindsey, grinned, and took off the "Columbia PD" baseball cap to reveal a freshly-shaved head.

"What happened to your hair?" exclaimed Lindsey.

"Got it shaved off. You like it?"

"It will take some getting used to," she said.

"What are you doing here?" asked Elton.

"We need to let you know that Margaret Carswell may be missing," she said. The desk sergeant, the dispatcher, Lindsey and Boulder gathered around a table. Lindsey and Boulder told them about J.B. Conner and the letters to Maggie, the dinner at Maggie's house and Boulder's finding out that Conner had a police record that mostly involved fraud. The desk sergeant took lots of notes. At the end of the conference, the desk sergeant instructed Elton to put out a bulletin to the Columbia Police Department and the Marion County Sheriff's Department to be on the lookout for a late-model red Corvette occupied by a male and a female. Elton did so. "Male subject is wanted for questioning regarding fraud case," Elton said into the dispatch microphone.

Afterwards, Lindsey went back to work at the Lampton Company. Boulder walked her back, then returned to the police department, where he hung around for four hours swapping war stories with the desk sergeant. At 4:30 p.m. there was a shift change at the station. Boulder decided he would go back downtown and kill time until Lindsey got off work. Just as he was about to walk out the door, there was a radio transmission from a Columbia Police Department officer.

"Go ahead, Unit 7," barked Elton.

"Ten-four, this is Unit 7," crackled the speaker beside the dispatcher. "I'm a half-block from Ms. Carswell's house at this time. Be advised that a red Corvette is now pulling into the driveway."

Chapter 17

The police officer remained a half-block from the Carswell house and observed a man and woman get out of the Corvette and go inside the house. The officer reported that there appeared to be nothing unusual. Boulder convinced the desk sergeant that there was no need for a police presence at this point, but that he would immediately contact the department if needed. Boulder then drove directly to the house, ascended the stairs to the front porch, and knocked on the door. Maggie opened it within a few seconds.

"Why Mr. Boulder," she said. "What a pleasant surprise. What are you doing here?"

"Some people have been worried about you," he said. "They didn't know where you had been all day. I just wanted to make certain that you were all right."

"I'm fine," she replied. "Please come in." She ushered him into the living room, where J.B. Conner was sitting on the sofa. He did not get up. "J.B. and I just got back from New Orleans. We spent the whole day on one street, I'm afraid. And it wasn't Bourbon Street either. It was Royale Street. We went from one antique store to another. I confess that I am now pooped with a capital P."

"Maggie, could I talk to you alone?" asked Boulder. "I have developed some more information that needs to come to your attention."

"You can tell me anything in front of J.B.," she said. "I have nothing to hide from him."

Boulder knew the look of a woman falling in love. At least she thought it was love. He could sense a new radiance about her, a smile in her voice and a life in her that wasn't there when he first met her. Conner was obviously working his charms on her. If she wanted him to tell her everything in front of the con man sitting on the sofa, that was fine with him.

"Very well," said Boulder. "If you insist. As part of my background investigation concerning Mr. Conner, I have discovered that he has been arrested and even has served time for certain criminal acts." Conner stood up and placed his hands on his hips. Boulder raised his arm, pointed his finger at Conner and said, "He told me that he wanted to pay you back for good deeds done to him and his family when they lived in a house owned by your husband. The fact of the matter is that Mr. Conner here swore to get even with your husband for making the family move. I won't go into the details. Perhaps Mr. Conner would care to change his story now."

Conner just stood there, a slight blushing about the ears becoming obvious. He crossed his arms in front of his chest and stared directly into Boulder's eyes.

"He told me that you would say all that," said Maggie.

"What?"

"I said that he told me you would say all that. He told me everything, so unless you have something else,

I would prefer to be alone with J.B."

"Maggie," said Boulder firmly. "I will leave right now if you will tell me one-on-one, just me and you alone, that you want me to go."

Conner walked around the coffee table and stood beside Boulder. He reached up and patted him on the back. There was a polite smile on his face. "I really think it's time for you to go. Maggie and I have a lot more to talk about tonight. Don't we, dear?"

Boulder didn't move a muscle. He looked directly at Margaret Carswell. The sound of silence grew louder. Finally, Maggie headed toward the front door.

"Allow me to walk you to the front door, Mr. Boulder," she said. "You can tell me whatever you will on the front porch, then you can go back to Jackson. I appreciate your good work and concern, but I no longer need your services. You can consider yourself discharged."

Boulder and Maggie walked to the front door. Conner turned and walked into the kitchen. As they stepped onto the front porch, Boulder stopped and said in a low voice, "Maggie, are you okay? This guy is a con man. He may even be wanted by the police right now."

"Would that be possible?"

"It could be," said Boulder. "I'm just worried about you. That's all."

"Mr. Boulder, it's been a long time since anyone has treated me the way that he has."

"I know," said Boulder. "That's all part of his act."

"But he likes me. I can tell. I think he may even love me."

"Would you come down to the police department and look at what they have? They are checking to see if he is a wanted man. They also have a copy of his record if you want to see it."

"Oh, my goodness," she said. She raised her hand to her forehead. "Now I'm getting all confused."

"Just tell him that you will be right back."

"Well, okay," she said, opening the front door. "J.B.," she said loudly to the inside of the house. "I'm going with Mr. Boulder, but I'll be back in a few minutes. Just sit tight."

She turned to Boulder and they began to walk down the front steps. At the same time they heard the loud steps of J.B. Conner hitting the floor inside and coming toward them. Suddenly the front door flung open and Conner barged out, yelling, "Wait!"

What happened next would later be heatedly debated. According to Conner, he hurriedly ran out onto the porch to tell Maggie that he wanted to go with them and accidentally ran into Maggie. Boulder would forever believe that Conner intentionally pushed her. In any event, Maggie tumbled violently down the steps, hit her head on the concrete sidewalk, and then lay unconscious on the ground in a face-down position. Boulder sprang to her and attempted to locate her pulse, while Conner just stood there saying, "No, Maggie, no!"

Boulder looked back up at him and ordered, "Go call an ambulance."

Chapter 18

Friends and family of Margaret Carswell gathered in the emergency room lobby of the hospital. Jack Boulder and J.B. Conner assumed positions near walls on opposite sides of the room, each choosing to blend into the background. In the middle of the lobby were Maggie's children, John, Jr. and Joanna, along with Junior's wife and son. The pastor of the First United Methodist Church had just walked into the room, and was being briefed by John, Jr. At this point the only thing known by everyone in the room was that Margaret Carswell had fallen down the front steps of her home and was taken to the hospital unconscious. An hour and twenty minutes had since elapsed.

Lindsey Plummer, in response to a telephone call from Boulder, arrived breathlessly. She walked in and looked around, searching frantically for the private investigator. When she saw him she rushed to him and asked what had happened. Boulder gave his version of the episode. Lindsey scanned the room again and upon finding J.B. Conner, glared menacingly at him.

Twenty minutes later a woman in green hospital scrubs entered from the double doors of the emergency treatment room hallway. She had a stethoscope around her neck. A nametag on her pocket read, "L.R. Dawson, MD."

"I understand Ms. Carswell's children are here," she

announced with a raised chin. John and Joanna Carswell stepped forward. "Come with me, please."

She led them through the double doors. Through a one-foot-square pane of glass in one of the doors, the rest of the crowd could discern that the doctor was talking to them in the hallway. As the doctor talked, Margaret Carswell's two children nodded their heads in response. Soon, they returned to the lobby and reported that Maggie had suffered a concussion and a broken left shoulder, and would be admitted to the hospital for further observation. She was now awake, but groggy and could not receive visitors until tomorrow morning. Those gathered all breathed a sigh of relief and more than one "thank goodness" was heard. John Carswell also let it be known that he and his sister would take turns staying with Maggie through the night.

Chapter 19

Maggie Carswell was released from the hospital on the day after Christmas. The weather turned bitter cold that day and the forecast called for below freezing temperatures that evening. She went home with her shoulder in a sling and a device that served as a cast around her shoulder. During her first day at home she was attended by John, Jr.'s wife Sharon, who efficiently, though reluctantly, handled Maggie's needs. Maggie insisted that she get right back to her normal schedule. She had visitors from her Sunday School class who brought dishes of food. Daughter Joanna came over and spent an uneventful night with her. Maggie even woke up the next morning before her daughter did. She didn't want to miss "The Today Show." Joanna was replaced by Sharon Carswell, who said that she was planning on spending all day at Maggie's home. At mid-morning, J.B. Conner showed up on the front porch.

"Good morning," he said to Sharon, who was standing inside behind the screen door. "You probably don't remember me. Everything was so confused at the hospital the other night. I'm J.B. Conner here to see Maggie."

From the back room Maggie called, "Is that you, J.B.? Come in. Come in."

Sharon opened the door and stepped back. Conner,

dressed in his usual western attire, stepped across the threshold and was immediately embraced with one arm by Maggie. Sharon looked on with mild surprise, not only at the display of affection, but also the renewed spirit of her mother-in-law.

"Mind if I talk to Maggie alone?" Conner asked Sharon.

"Of course she doesn't," said Maggie. "Sharon, if you don't mind."

Sharon departed for the kitchen. Conner and Maggie sat side-by-side on the sofa and talked in hushed voices. Soon Sharon was summoned from the kitchen.

"Sharon," said Maggie. "You can leave now. J.B. will be staying with me. He can take care of me. Besides, you've got a child to tend to and things to do at the country club."

Maggie seemed determined in spite of Sharon's mild protests, so Sharon departed. She went straight to her husband's office and told him what had happened. John, Jr. did not take the news well. He proceeded purposefully to his mother's home to verify what his wife had told him. He found his mother sitting in a chair in the living room, wearing a heavy robe and slippers. J.B. Conner sat on the sofa as if he were a relative visiting from out of town.

"If you don't mind," John, Jr. told Conner. "I'd like to talk to her alone."

"Sure enough," said Conner, as he picked up a cup of hot chocolate that was setting on the coffee table. "I'll be in the kitchen," he said to Maggie.

"Mother, what's this I hear about this man, Mr. Conner, taking care of you?" asked John, Jr. "We have already made plans for round-the-clock sitters to be here."

"I'll have no such thing," insisted Maggie. "I don't need any sitters. As you can see, I get around just fine. All I have is a broken shoulder."

"Mother, who is this man? Do you really know him?"

"I know all I need to know," she said. "Now you go back to work and take care of your family. I think your wife needs some attention."

"What does that mean?"

"Good-bye, John, Junior."

For the next four weeks, J.B. Conner arrived in his Corvette at 6:00 a.m. every morning and left at 10:30 p.m. every night. Although Maggie received visitors during the day, she asked them to leave after a short while. The talk around the church was that Maggie had changed, and that it was probably due to her head injury. Others gossiped about the man in the red Corvette who was all but living at Maggie's home.

Chapter 20

Lindsey Plummer smiled down at her young son, who lay on his stomach in contented slumber. She pulled the blue flannel blanket up to the base of his head and leaned over into the crib and kissed him one more time before turning out the light. The marriage to her son's father had been a painful mistake, but was more than made up for in the love she felt for the little fellow in front of her. There was only one bedroom in her apartment, so she used it as her room and the baby's room. At first, it had been hard for her to put the baby in the crib at night, instead of letting him sleep in her bed. The crib was what the experts recommended, and she intuitively knew they were right. It didn't make it any easier. A mother and her baby need to be together.

She retreated to her small living room and began reading a political science textbook. The new semester had just begun, and she needed to maintain her perfect average. After a few moments, she realized that she did not remember the last paragraph she had read. Her mind was preoccupied with something else. She could not keep from thinking about Maggie and J.B. Conner. She worried that Conner may be doing to Maggie Carswell what her ex-husband had done to her—taking her for a ride. There could be pain and suffering. She wondered if Maggie could handle it if the worst happened. She had talked to Maggie on the telephone at least every other day since her injury. Maggie seemed as happy as she could be. She talked like a high school girl in love. Even Lindsey knew that girls in love are often blinded by it. Something told her that it was time to act. She put down her book, called her mother next door, and asked if she could watch the baby for an hour. Her mother was there in five minutes. Lindsey drove straight to Maggie's house.

When she arrived, Maggie warmly welcomed her. Maggie wore black slacks and a bright red, heavy cotton sweater with white snowflake designs. Her arm was still in a sling, but she looked really good. It was the first time Lindsey had ever seen Maggie dressed in anything other than a dress. J.B. Conner was sitting on the couch with an Outdoor Life magazine in his hands. The fireplace was lit. The scene looked peaceful and cozy.

"Miz Maggie," said Lindsey. "I'm so sorry to bother you like this, but I wonder if I could get your advice about a personal problem I am having."

"Of course," replied Maggie, sensing a need in Lindsey for a friend and some talking time. She turned to Conner and said, "J.B., would you mind taking care of that little grocery list on the kitchen table."

He read her mind and said, "I'd be proud to. It may be forty-five minutes before I get back though. I'm gonna go by the Wal-Mart and check out the new fishing gear." He got the list and a heavy jacket and departed.

"Follow me to the kitchen," said Maggie. "We need

some hot chocolate."

"You and your hot chocolate," quipped Lindsey with a teasing laugh.

"Hot chocolate warms the body and the soul."

A few minutes later they were back in the living room sitting by the fireplace, mugs of hot chocolate in hand. Lindsey cleared her throat and began to speak.

"Wait a minute," said Maggie. "Is this about me or about you?"

"I'm afraid it's about the concern that I have for you."

"I see," Maggie said with a hum. "Let me see if I can get you started. You are worried that I don't know what I'm getting into and that J.B. is just using me. Is that it?"

"How did you know?"

"That's what everybody is worried about," said Maggie. "Everybody who comes by here wants to tell me something. I'm darn near wearing out the floor between the living room and the kitchen from people wanting to give me advice."

"We're just concerned. That's all."

"I know. And I appreciate it. I really do. But I think I know what I'm doing."

"What about his record?" asked Lindsey.

"That's a good question," she said, pausing to reach over with her good arm and pick up the mug of hot chocolate. "He has convinced me that those things are in the past and were mostly mistakes. He grew up awfully poor, you know."

"That's no excuse," said Lindsey. "I'm poor and I don't break the law."

"You have people who care about you. That's something he never had."

"And I care about you," said Lindsey, almost pleading. "I'm just afraid you are going to get hurt. You are so different from him."

"Opposites attract is what they say."

"I know," said the young girl. "But you two are really opposite. How do you get in and out of that Corvette, anyway?"

She laughed. "Not easily, I can tell you."

Lindsey got serious. "Why are you doing this? It's not like you. Something else is causing this. Please be honest with me. That's all I ask. Then I'll leave and won't bother you any more."

Maggie leaned forward. "Very well. I'll tell you. I'm angry, that's why. Angry because everybody treats me like an old lady. Well, I'm not an old lady." Her voice grew louder. "My life is just beginning. I've found someone who treats me like a young lady. Maybe he is trying to take advantage of me. If so, he's doing a good job of it, because I feel young when I'm with him. You don't know what it's like to be treated like an old person. You don't know what it's like when your children and grandchildren don't even want to spend time with you. You don't know what it's like to have people just waiting for you to die. When you know all those things, then you can come back and tell me how concerned you are. But for now, please leave me alone and let me live my life!"

As soon as she uttered the last sentence, she was sorry. The tears began to form in both Maggie's and Lindsey's eyes. Lindsey jumped up and ran out the door, leaving it wide open. She dashed down the steps, got in her car and drove away. Maggie stood at the front door, tears flowing. The cold wind brushed her face, and she began to recover. She closed the door and went back inside.

"They just don't understand," she thought to herself. "They just don't understand."

Chapter 21

John, Jr. and his sister Joanna met at the law office on the Thursday of the fifth week of their mother's recuperation. Things were not going right. Mother was not acting like herself. But John, Jr. was confident that things were going to work out in their favor.

"How can you be so sure that Mother is not going to run off with this guy and get married?" Joanna asked of her brother.

"I have some good news, my dear sister," he replied. "I did some checking into Mr. Conner and found that he has a record."

"That's not going to phase Mother. She always took in strays. After all, the guy has been at her house for weeks now."

"I'm not going to tell Mother about his past," said John. "I've got another idea."

"Well, it had better be a good one."

Later that evening, J.B. Conner kissed Maggie Carswell on the cheek before he left her home. He got in his red Corvette and drove off toward downtown. He turned left onto Main Street, his thoughts only of Maggie. He did not notice the car behind him. As Conner's Corvette drove by the front of the Marion County Courthouse, headlights from the car behind him blinked back and forth from low beam to high beam. He pulled over and stopped in the parking area on the east side of the courthouse. He reached down under his seat and fondled the .38 caliber Smith & Wesson revolver, then picked it up and let it rest on the seat between his legs. All he could see behind him was the bright headlights of a large car. One of the lights darkened and a shadow was created as someone walked into the light. That someone was approaching.

"Mr. Conner?" He didn't recognize the voice.

"Yeah," he replied.

"Would you mind stepping out of the car?"

"Who are you? A cop of some kind? Show me a badge."

"I'm Margaret Carswell's son."

"Oh, yeah," said Conner, getting out of his car and leaving the gun on the seat. "I recognize you now." He got out of the car. The two of them stood between their cars, the scene illuminated by city street lights.

"Conner, I've got a message for you," said Carswell. "In my pocket is a proposed peace bond. I'm going to file it tomorrow with the Justice Court. I don't think the judge will have any hesitation protecting a solid citizen from a scoundrel with a record for fraud and cheating. You will be forbidden to get within sixty feet of my mother. I suggest you get back inside your little red Corvette and not come back to Columbia any time soon. Otherwise, you may find yourself a guest in our city jail. Do I make myself clear?"

"Clear as a bell," said Conner, snidely. "Clear as a bell." He got in his car and drove away.

Chapter 22

At 4:00 p.m. the next day the secretary to John Carswell, Jr. informed him that the most prominent lawyer in Columbia was holding on line one. He picked up the receiver with prideful anticipation. Just last month he had been asked to consider serving as an officer with the local bar association. This was probably the call informing him that the nominating committee had chosen him.

"Good afternoon," he answered with a smile. "Is this windy, February day cold enough for you?"

"John, could you be in my office at nine o'clock tomorrow morning? There will be a conference regarding a matter that affects you personally and directly," the most prominent lawyer said in formal, businesslike fashion.

"Well, sure. What's this about?"

"Thank you. We look forward to seeing you then." There was a click. Not even a good-bye.

He felt his face go flush as he considered the possibilities inherent in such a telephone call. There was no doubt in his mind that this had something to do with J.B. Conner. He had detected a key word in the telephone conversation, and that word was "personally." What had Conner done? How could he have gotten the most prominent lawyer in Columbia to represent him? Had Conner gotten some kind of injunction against him?

The questions kept filling his head like rain pouring from a roof into a gutter that couldn't hold the overflow. He picked up the telephone and dialed his mother's number. She could shed some light on this. There was no answer.

Ten minutes later Joanna Carswell received a similar call while she was walking at 4.5 miles an hour on the treadmill in her bedroom. Afterwards, she considered calling her brother to see if he recommended she have a lawyer with her, but she decided that her brother was the last person she would go to for legal advice. It would be better to go to the meeting and get information before overreacting. She guessed that it was related to a school matter. The school was probably represented by the most prominent lawyer in Columbia. Maybe a lawsuit had been filed by one of the students. On the other hand, her brother might have some insight. She dialed his office.

"Hi, Joanna," said John, Jr. after being told his sister was on the line. "I was just about to call you."

"Why?"

"Something has come up, I'm afraid," he said. "I think that it might have something to do with mother."

"Did you get a call from a high-powered attorney requesting a meeting tomorrow morning?" she asked.

"I did," he replied, suddenly feeling the onrush of a panic attack.

"So did I," she said. "What do you think it means?"

"It obviously means that she's gotten a lawyer."

"For what reason?" she asked.

"I don't know, but the one she's got is one tough customer."

"This doesn't sound like a routine meeting," she said. "He talked to me like I was someone going before a grand jury. Have you done anything?"

"What do you mean?"

"You said you had a plan. Remember?"

"Yes," he said. "But there's nothing to worry about. Just show up and let me do the talking."

Jack Boulder and Lindsey Plummer also received calls requesting their presence at a meeting that had been requested by Maggie Carswell. Each assured the caller that they would be in attendance.

Chapter 23

The next morning six people sat down around the lawyer's large table in the conference room. There was the attorney who called the meeting, his secretary, John Carswell, Jr., Joanna Carswell, Lindsey Plummer and Jack Boulder. In front of the secretary was a standard cassette player.

"Thank you all for coming," said the attorney. "I represent Margaret Carswell, whom all of you either know or are related to. She has made some special plans and asked me to facilitate the communication of those plans to you." He nodded at the secretary, who turned on the cassette recorder.

"By now, you probably know that J.B. and I got married," Maggie's voice proclaimed proudly.

The reactions around the table were mixed. John Carswell, Jr. was stunned. The color drained from his face, and he stared at the device in disbelief as if seeking the answer to that most frustrating of all questions—why did she do this? His sister's lips displayed a Mona Lisa smile, the kind used by two women who share a deep secret. Her eyes cut over to her brother, and she glared at him as if he were one of her schoolboys who had gotten caught red handed with contraband in his pocket. A tight-lipped smile came across Lindsey's face, but inside there was a grin as big as an early summer Marion County watermelon. Boulder moved his eyes from person to person, observing the reactions. The attorney and his secretary sat expressionless. The tape continued.

"I expect this comes as a big disappointment to John, Jr., who is right now worrying that he is not going to inherit a lot of money." All eyes cut to John, Jr. "By the way, John, I am taping this in case you have any ideas about my sanity in the drawing up of my will." There was a pause. "Yes, I have drawn up my will, and it is as follows: First, enough money has been set aside to educate my two grandchildren through college. John, the worst thing I could do to you is leave you a lot of money. You need to learn how to live on your own without borrowing from your sister." John, Jr. threw a glare at Joanna, who mirrored it right back. "Since you are my son, I am leaving you $25,000." Four sets of eyes cut to John for his reaction. There was none.

"Next. To my daughter Joanna, who has served her community well as a teacher, I leave the sum of one hundred thousand dollars. The remainder of my estate

will be left to various community organizations, especially the Main Street program. I believe strongly in what it is doing for downtown Columbia.

"Now let me tell you the story about J.B. He originally planned to marry me for my money and to get even with my former husband through me. He also told me what my husband did to his family. He says that his plans were foiled when he fell in love with me. Frankly, I don't know if he's telling the truth or not. All I know is that I am feeling better than I have felt in a long time and it's all because of him. I feel that somebody cares for me, and me alone. Likewise, he has had no one to care for him, and now he does. But you'll be happy to know that I had that lawyer in front of you draw up a pre-nuptial agreement that makes certain that all he gets is me, and nothing else. I don't know how it's all going to work out, but I'm enjoying it, and . . . well, we'll see.

"Lindsey, I apologize for the way I treated you the other night. I care for you deeply and did not mean to hurt you. I hope you will forgive me." Lindsey nodded her head as tears welled up in her eyes. "J.B. and I are moving to Florida. He bought us a condominium down there and got a new job managing one of the biggest mobile home companies in the Florida Panhandle. So I won't be needing that big old house on Church Street. Lindsey, I would like to rent it to you and your mother for five dollars a month, if you would like to live in it. It's a good house and it needs a good person like you to be in it. Your little boy would like the big yard and the white squirrels. If you find that the house suits you, I would be glad to sell it to you for an amount that you could afford. The lawyer will inform you of the price.

"Finally, Mr. Boulder, I have something to say to you. You did a good job finding your man. You also found a good man. I know you don't believe that, but I hope you will realize you are wrong. Anyway, I appreciate your concern for me. There's a check for your services with the attorney.

"So that's all I have to say. Wish me luck. I hope I'm doing the right thing. But like that Pearl River we all know, everything flows on to something else down stream. God bless all of you."

The secretary turned off the cassette player, and the attorney at the head of the table went right to business. He handed Jack Boulder an envelope.

"Here's your compensation, Mr. Boulder," he said, then reached for a legal-sized document on the table. "Here is the lease agreement referred to by Ms. Carswell. Ms. Plummer, is this something you think will be of interest to you?"

"Oh, yes!" said Lindsey. "Most definitely."

"Wait a minute," interjected John Carswell. "You know as well as I do that that deed and any sale to her would fail for lack of consideration."

"Do you want to challenge the conveyance?" asked the attorney.

"No, but . . ."

"Then respect the wishes of your mother, John," he

said firmly.

"Oh, there is one other thing, as it relates to Ms. Plummer," said the attorney. "Ms. Carswell appreciates all the work you are putting in to earn your degree. She has set up a fund that I am to administrate to see that all of your expenses are paid toward your college degree."

"Oh, my goodness," said Lindsey, brushing back the tears. "I'm speechless. Thank you so much."

"It's Maggie you have to thank," the attorney responded. And now, if there are no more questions, there is a matter at the courthouse that requires my attention."